W9-CBV-656

The Tooth Fairy

Written by Kirsten Hall
Illustrated by Dawn Apperley

My First
READER

children's press®

A Division of Scholastic Inc.

New York Toronto London Auckland Sydney
Mexico City New Delhi Hong Kong
Danbury, Connecticut

Library of Congress Cataloging-in-Publication Data

Hall, Kirsten.
  The tooth fairy / written by Kirsten Hall ; illustrated by Dawn
Apperley.– 1st American ed.
        p. cm. – (My first reader)
Summary: When he loses a tooth, a young boy excitedly awaits a visit
from the tooth fairy.
  ISBN 0-516-22938-9 (lib. bdg.)   0-516-24640-2 (pbk.)
  [1. Teeth–Fiction. 2. Tooth fairy–Fiction. 3. Stories in rhyme.] I.
Apperley, Dawn, ill. II. Title. III. Series.
  PZ8.3.H146To 2003
  [E]–dc21
                              2003003694

Text © 1994 Nancy Hall, Inc.
Illustrations © 2003 Dawn Apperley
Published in 2003 by Children's Press
A Division of Scholastic Inc.
All rights reserved. Published simultaneously in Canada.
Printed in China.

CHILDREN'S PRESS and associated logos are trademarks and or registered trademarks of Scholastic Library Publishing.
SCHOLASTIC and associated logos are trademarks and or registered trademarks of Scholastic Inc.

17 18 19 R 21 20 19 18   62
Scholastic Inc., 557 Broadway, New York, NY 10012.

Note to Parents and Teachers

Once a reader can recognize and identify the 34 words
used to tell this story, he or she will be able to read successfully
the entire book. These 34 words are repeated throughout the story,
so that young readers will be able to easily recognize
the words and understand their meaning.

The 34 words used in this book are:

be	here	open	tight
bed	I'll	out	time
close	it	pass	to
clouds	it's	she'll	tonight
come	keep	soon	tooth
eyes	look	stars	up
fairy	moon	surprises	will
fell	my	the	
go	near	them	

My tooth fell out.

Look here!

Look here!

I'll go to bed.

I'll keep it near.

I'll close my eyes.

I'll close them tight!

17

The tooth fairy
will come tonight.

She'll pass the stars.

She'll pass the moon.

She'll pass the clouds.

She'll be here soon.

It's time to open up my eyes!

It's time to open my surprise!

ABOUT THE AUTHOR

Kirsten Hall has lived most of her life in New York City. While she was still in high school, she published her first book for children, *Bunny, Bunny*. Since then, she has written and published more than sixty children's books. A former early education teacher, Kirsten currently works as a children's book editor.

ABOUT THE ILLUSTRATOR

Dawn Apperley studied graphic design in college and began illustrating children's books as soon as she graduated. Born in England, she has lived in the United States and Spain. Apperley enjoys cycling, inline skating, and gardening. She currently lives in London with her small white rabbit, Coco.